To Bob and Jill

BLASTING INTO THE PAST

M. D. Spenser

Paradise Press, Inc.

Weston, FL

32124-5

Published by Paradise Press, Inc. by arrangement with River Publishing, Inc. All right, title and interest to the "HUMANOMORPHS" logo and design are owned by River Publishing, Inc. No portion of the "HUMANOMORPHS" logo and design may be reproduced in part or whole without prior written permission from River Publishing, Inc. An application for a registered trademark of the "HUMANO-MORPHS" logo and design is pending with the Federal Patent and Trademark office.

ISBN 1-57657-335-4

EXCLUSIVE DISTRIBUTION BY PARADISE PRESS, INC.

Cover Dsign & Illustrations by Nicholas Forder

Printed in the U.S.A.

Chapter One

I hate history!

Hate, hate, hate history lessons!

It isn't that I dislike school — not at all. School has always been fun for me. Everybody always tells me I'm one of the "brainy" kids in the class.

You know the type.

I guess it's true. I almost always get As on tests and I'm often the first kid to answer the teacher's questions about literature and math and science.

I especially love science — chemistry is my favorite.

Learning new things is pretty awesome, you know?

But something about history lessons always makes me want to run from our class and throw up all over the bathroom. The funniest thing about it is, I can never explain exactly *why* I feel this way.

1

All I know is that it seems to have some strange connection with our teacher, Mr. Wicker.

He's a nice teacher — most of the time, anyway. Maybe a little odd-looking, sure. But who am I to criticize anyone for that?

I'm not exactly going to win any prizes for being the most handsome boy in school, that's for sure!

Mr. Wicker is very tall and very skinny, with thin black hair greased straight back. He has a tiny mustache and a stubby, crooked nose, and his pants are too short.

And his clothes are always black. Entirely black.

Pretty weird for a teacher!

But the oddest thing about Mr. Wicker is that he seems to like me fine all day long — until our history lessons begin.

"Very good, Benjamin! You'll be a famous chemist someday," he often says when I answer a science problem correctly.

He says this in front of the whole class, too. I like that, though it's kind of embarrassing, too.

But somehow whenever we start to talk about history, Mr. Wicker's attitude suddenly changes. His dark eyes get a funny look in them, as if he's angry.

Very angry — at *me*!

He never smiles at me during history. And he says strange things to me. Only to me, as though I've done something wrong.

That's just what things were like on this one afternoon in November — the same afternoon when all the miserable troubles started for my family.

Mr. Wicker began giving our class a history lesson at the end of the day, as usual. He had been smiling and laughing and cracking jokes with the other kids and me all afternoon.

You know how it is with teachers sometimes — he seemed in a really good mood.

Then he said those awful words I dreaded every day.

"OK, let's all open our history books now," Mr. Wicker said, suddenly glaring at me. "And I hope you've all done your homework!"

Only, I hadn't done my homework. Like I explained before, I hate history!

And I could tell that Mr. Wicker *knew* I hadn't done my homework.

"Let's start with — oh, why don't we begin with Benjamin," he said, emphasizing my name. "Benjamin, will you tell us what great evil in this country was a major cause of our Civil War? I'm sure you read your homework assignment last night, hmmmm?"

Mr. Wicker had been looking down at the book in his hands until he came to that last word. Then he had looked up at me with an expression that I found frightening when he said that one word: "hmmmm?"

It was creepy, though I had seen that look many times before. There was something in his eyes. But no one else in my class ever seemed to notice this.

Not even my best pal, Taylor, who sat right next to me.

I noticed it, though. Mr. Wicker's eyes looked far away, as though he was remembering something horrible and painful. At the same time his eyes seemed furious — almost red with hatred and disgust!

To me, they looked like the eyes of some killer maniac!

Why? Why did he hate me during every history class?

That look in his eyes made my stomach ache

and my blood run cold. I prayed each night never to see that look again.

It always made me feel as if Mr. Wicker actually wanted to hurt me! My own teacher looked as if he wanted to wrap something tight around my throat and strangle me!

"Uh, well . . . sure, yeah, I read my homework, of course," I lied.

"Then be good enough to tell the class what you read about last night in your history book, Benjamin," he replied with a nasty smile.

"OK, sure. Well, uh . . . uh, well there was this thing. Uh, and it was, well . . . it was pretty bad and the North and the South decided they had to get rid of it except . . . " I stammered.

"Enough!" Mr. Wicker interrupted angrily, slamming his book on a desk. "I think we can all see that you haven't read your homework! If you had, you would know about this major reason for the War Between the States. Maybe someone else can tell Benjamin. Yes, Patty?"

"It was slavery, Mr. Wicker," Patty answered smugly, turning around in her seat to sneer at me —

me, the smart kid who had given the dumb answer. "I did my homework assignment last night, just like you told us."

"Very good, Patty! Yes, you're right. Slavery is the correct answer," Mr. Wicker said, scowling at me. "Slavery has been a terrible, terrible problem around the world for many centuries. Once it was a problem in our own country. Wealthy farmers in the South actually owned other people! Can you believe that? Owned black people as if they were cattle or horses or sheep. And the farmers sometimes kept these slaves in chains and sometimes whipped them until they bled."

Mr. Wicker was still looking right at me as he talked.

"Oh, and sometimes they killed the slaves too, right?" Patty added.

"Yes, Patty. You're right. That's what they did to slaves who didn't obey the rules, and to slaves who didn't do what they were told," Mr. Wicker said. He walked over to my side and glared down at me with the expression of a cold-hearted murderer. "Punishment! Severe, brutal punishment! Swift, cruel punishment! That's what slavery was like. Do you understand me,

Benjamin?"

"Uh, y-y-yes," I said, even though I didn't understand why he was saying this to me.

"And punishment is also what happens to children who don't read their homework lessons, isn't it?" he continued, his eyes wide and crazy. "You will stay after history class when the rest of your schoolmates are through, Benjamin. Yes, just you and me here in our little room. Alone! Hmmm? And we will learn about punishment together! Do you understand me, young man? You will learn more about brutal punishment than you ever wanted to know!"

Chapter Two

School was over.

I was in the classroom. Alone with Mr. Wicker.

After the other kids had gone, my teacher had flicked off the lights in the room. Then he had started to slowly walk around my desk, circling me like a hungry shark.

It was really, really weird! Spooky!

I couldn't understand why he seemed so angry. What was it about the history lessons that always turned him against me?

"Mr. Wackerman, sit up straight!" he suddenly barked at me.

Wackerman is my last name, by the way. Benjamin Wackerman, that's me. I always knew I was in real trouble when Mr. Wicker used my last name like that.

"Fat people such as yourself should know better, Mr. Wackerman!" my teacher went on. "You look like a lumpy potato on a grocery shelf when you slouch in your chair! It's most disgusting!"

I was really surprised he called me fat. And disgusting, too!

My teacher had never insulted my appearance before. Like I told you, he wasn't exactly God's gift to beauty himself.

When he said those things, I understood that he must really be extra mad!

True, I may look kind of geeky, I guess.

And OK, maybe I'm a little pudgy. Some of the meaner kids call me fatso. I have wiry black hair that sticks up in the back of my head, like a tuft of burned grass.

But so what? There's nothing wrong with that, you know?

Only the stupid, nasty kids at school make fun of me for the way I look. And I don't want them for friends anyway.

I have one true friend — Taylor.

He's a great guy, tall and strong and loyal. He doesn't care what anyone says about me. He stays my friend, no matter what.

As I sat in the classroom with my teacher, I sure wished Taylor was by my side!

Things were getting weirder every second. Mr. Wicker continued talking.

"You seem surprised that I kept you here after class, Benjamin," he said, speaking each word slowly. "But I'm your teacher and it's my right. It's my right as your custodian, the keeper of your mind during each school day."

"Y-yes, sir," I replied, not wanting to make him any angrier.

"So you shouldn't be surprised. No, not at all! Because you're mine for several hours every day. You and all the others in my class," Mr. Wicker intoned, his eyes growing wild again. "You are my responsibility, don't you see? I control you during that time. I own you!"

"Uh, o-own us, s- sir?" I stammered.

"Yes, of course! Your mind, boy! I own your mind! And it makes me very angry — very angry *indeed* — when one of you fails to do what I tell you to do! There must be penalties for that! Punishment, Mr.

Wackerman! Hmmmm?"

"P-p-punishment?"

Mr. Wicker was behind me, standing so near my back that I couldn't even see him by turning my head. But I could feel his warm, bad-smelling breath all over me. And I knew that his eyes were glaring down in a red rage.

"Yes, because this can't be allowed to continue," he said. "It simply can't be allowed because some day you'll be a fine scientist and so I must stop you from doing this now. *Now*, Benjamin!"

I didn't have any clue what he meant. It all sounded so strange.

Stop me? From doing what?

I didn't know what he meant — not for another instant, anyway.

Not until I felt his fingers very slowly starting to circle my throat from behind! That's when everything was clear to me in a terrifying flash!

Mr. Wicker really did want to hurt me, after all! He was going to do it right here, in this dark classroom!

My teacher was going to choke me to death!

Chapter Three

I tried to leap out of my chair.

But Mr. Wicker had a tight grip on my throat!

I tried to scream, but I couldn't. He was squeezing my windpipe too tightly for that!

This was insane! Completely crazy!

A skinny, nerdy-looking teacher was going to murder me right in the middle of the school! For no reason at all!

And there was nothing I could do about it!

"Heughlph!" I said.

I was trying to scream the word "help," of course, but it came out all twisted. And it was too soft for anyone to hear, sounding like a squeak from a rusty door.

"I must end this now! Now, Mr. Wackerman, don't you see?" Mr. Wicker said furiously. "Now! Finally end all of this! You are too dangerous for me to let you live!"

"Heughlph!" I gurgled again.

"I'm sorry! I'm very sorry but it's necessary! You've been a terrible threat for too long!" he rambled insanely. "I'm sorry, so sorry but I must do this! I must!"

I could hardly breathe and I was growing faint from lack of oxygen. As any good scientist knows, the cells in the human body need oxygen to live. Soon I wouldn't have the strength to get away.

I was dying!

That's when I remembered that Mr. Wicker had a trick left knee. He had hurt it in a car accident years earlier and sometimes it made him limp a little.

He always joked that he could tell when rainstorms were coming because his knee ached from the humidity.

It seemed my only chance. I had to strike at his weakness! Somehow, I had to hit Mr. Wicker's bad knee!

But he was still in back of my chair, choking me from behind. What could I do?

Quickly, I swung my left leg to the side of my

desk. Then with all my might, I flung my foot backwards and up, hoping to hit his knee.

I used all my force, every ounce of muscle and fat in my body.

But I missed! My foot whiffed harmlessly through the air.

Now I was in even worse trouble.

Mr. Wicker went nutso! He howled like a wild animal and lifted me out of my chair by the throat!

It was almost like I was being executed by hanging — except the rope was my teacher's hands! Who would have imagined that such a skinny man could be so strong?

"You disgustin' monster!" Mr. Wicker shouted at me. "You will *die* for that, sir!"

My neck hurt worse than ever. I couldn't take even the smallest breath.

I struggled and wiggled against him with my last ounce of fight. It was no use.

But somehow I still noticed that Mr. Wicker's voice sounded strange. It sounded as if he had said, "You will *dah* for that, sir!"

I realized that he was talking with a Southern

14

accent. You know, like some guy from Alabama or Georgia or someplace like that.

As I inched closer to death one final thought flitted through my head: "This guy's totally, absolutely wacko! Mr. Wicker isn't from the South! He's from Maine!"

Chapter Four

The world was going gray.

I felt my eyes closing and my body going limp!

I was about to die!

Then without warning, I felt my body drop onto the floor like a rock. Mr. Wicker had released me.

Then I heard him scream in pain.

I was dazed from lack of O_2 — that's the chemical symbol for oxygen, of course. Oxygen is necessary to think clearly. Without it, you get all strange and wacky in the head, you know?

That's how I felt right then. Really fuzzy upstairs.

But as I came to, I could see Mr. Wicker lying on the floor, holding his bad left knee.

Slowly it started to make sense: I had accidentally kicked him when I was in my death throes. Just as I was ready to pass out for good, I had flailed my arms and legs around one last time.

And somehow I had nailed him, giving him a good knock on the knee!

Wow, talk about luck!

My head was just barely getting clearer. But it was clear enough to see that Mr. Wicker was staring at me in horror. My teacher looked as if he had just awakened from a nightmare.

"Benjamin! Benjamin, forgive me!" he pleaded, still sprawled on the floor. "I swear to you, I didn't mean you any harm! I was just trying to teach you a lesson. Please, Benjamin!"

"Mr. Wicker, I think you're totally nuts!" I shouted, struggling to my feet. "You just tried to kill me! You were talking with a Southern accent and strangling me!"

I hurried towards the door. I just wanted to get away from him.

"But Benjamin, you don't understand! Please believe me, I didn't want to cause you any harm!" Mr. Wicker said in a pitiful voice. "Please, I beg you, son! Don't turn me into the police! It's just that I . . . I couldn't help myself! I'm sorry, Benjamin!"

But I was already outside the classroom door. I started running home as fast as my chubby legs would carry me.

I couldn't wait to tell my parents. I knew they would call the police and then Mr. Wicker would go to jail, maybe for the rest of his life.

A crazy man like that shouldn't be allowed to teach kids, I thought as I ran. I hope they lock him up in prison and throw away the key!

I was puffing so hard from running that I almost felt like Mr. Wicker was choking me again. I could hardly draw a breath.

Somehow, I made it to my house and ran inside, praying that either Mom or Dad was home from work. They needed to hear about the attack as soon as possible.

They had to make sure Mr. Wicker didn't hurt any of my classmates, especially Taylor.

I was really lucky again, because both my parents were sitting in the living room with the TV news on.

"D-Dad, uh, M-Mom, uh, listen . . . " I panted. "Can you turn off the news? I have to talk to you guys!"

Dad turned to look at me. He was smiling.

"Hi there, Benny!" he said cheerfully.

Yeah, my parents call me Benny. Pretty goofy, huh?

"You're all out of breath, son. Sit down and watch TV with us," Dad suggested.

"Yes, we'll have dinner soon. Pizza, your favorite!" Mom added with a grin.

Didn't they hear me? Couldn't they see I was upset? What was wrong with them?

"No, no, no. Listen, you guys! You don't get it!" I spit out. "My teacher, Mr. Wicker — he tried to kill me! Honest he did! He almost choked me to death!"

They were looking at the TV screen, still smiling.

"Oh, really? Well, that's nice, dear," Mom answered sweetly.

I couldn't understand this. My parents always listened to me when I talked to them. But they weren't listening now.

"Mom! Dad!" I shouted. "Stop and pay attention to me! I almost bought the farm! My teacher tried to squeeze the life right out of me! Look at the marks on my neck! We need to call the police!"

My parents turned in their seats, with odd expressions on their faces. They seemed to stare at the red marks Mr. Wicker's hands had left on my neck.

They looked vaguely troubled but not shocked or angry. Didn't they understand me yet?

Couldn't they tell that someone had tried to strangle me?

"Why that's — well, that's just terrible," Mom replied without feeling. She said this in the same tone she would use to ask for the salt shaker during dinner. "We'll have to speak to him about that sometime."

"Yes, Benny. You go wash your hands and come join us, son. We'll talk to Mr. Wicker about this," Dad agreed. "I can't understand why he'd do such a thing to you."

Then they turned back to watch the TV news as if nothing at all had happened to me.

And both of them were smiling again.

Chapter Five

Things were no better the next morning.

In fact, they were worse. A *lot* worse!

Mom and Dad both said they understood what I'd been telling them over and over since the night before: that my teacher tried to kill me. But they still weren't at all upset about it.

Didn't my parents believe me? I had proof. I had bruises around my neck where Mr. Wicker choked me.

Why wouldn't they call the police? I mean, they didn't even call the school to tell our principal that a crazy man was teaching there. They didn't call anyone.

I was so angry I didn't know what to say to them. I sat at the breakfast table with a bowl of hot cereal in front of me. But I wasn't eating.

I just sulked, probably giving off more steam than my oatmeal.

Then I noticed something. Mom looked a little funny somehow. I couldn't figure out what was wrong, except she didn't seem quite the same.

Maybe it was that her pretty blond hair appeared — oh, I don't know — maybe a little gray. She had dark circles under her eyes. The lines on her face were just a bit deeper.

It was hard to tell exactly what was wrong. But my mother didn't look the way she usually did. It was almost as if she had aged fifteen years in one night.

I didn't understand how that was possible, but there had to be some logical explanation.

And she hadn't been acting like herself either.

Maybe she was sick.

"Mom, are you all right?" I asked.

"Yes, dear. Of course. Why do you ask?" she answered, smiling.

"I don't know. No reason, I guess," I said, staring at my cereal bowl.

I heard Dad bounding down the steps two at a time, the way he usually does before work. I felt relieved. Maybe he knew what was wrong with Mom.

Dad is like this almost every weekday morning

— pretty happy to go to work. He really loves his job as a doctor at a big hospital, even when he has some tough medical problem to solve.

There probably aren't many fathers who smile every day before they leave for work, but my dad does.

Then he came into the kitchen. And he wasn't smiling this morning.

"Where's my coffee? Can't you have my coffee ready when I come downstairs for work! Is that too much to ask?" he snarled at my mother.

"Yes, dear. I'm sorry," Mom said pleasantly. "I'll try to do better tomorrow."

"See that you do!" he snapped, grabbing the cup from her so quickly that hot coffee slopped all over his white sleeve. "Oh great! Look at this! Now I have to change shirts! Look what you've done!"

"I'm sorry, dear. Forgive me," Mom replied without emotion.

"What kind of idiot are you anyway?" Dad barked.

What was going on? Dad never talked to Mom this way, all angry and nasty. And Mom never acted so odd, as if she didn't care about anything.

Were my parents getting enough sleep? Were they taking their vitamins?

Maybe they both were just completely losing their cookies.

"D-Dad, do you feel all right?" I asked quietly. "Are you and Mom OK?"

"Fine! I feel fine, except for your mother spilling coffee on me!" he snapped. "That was a stupid question, Benny! Why would you ask me that?"

"No reason," I said, eating a spoonful of oatmeal so I didn't have to look at him.

Mom poured a new cup of coffee and held it out to Dad, but he brushed the cup aside without touching it.

"Oh, forget the coffee now! I'll just eat breakfast at the hospital! I can change shirts there too!" Dad said, almost yelling. "I have to do everything myself! Someone needs to crack the whip around this house! What we need here is some swift, severe discipline!"

With those words, Dad stormed out the back door muttering to himself. He roared away in his car, tires squealing.

Wow! I'd never seen him like that before.

He seemed so mean. And he was saying things like "swift, severe discipline" and "crack the whip." What was he talking about, anyway?

His words sounded an awful lot like Mr. Wicker's warning to me about after-school punishment.

But the strangest thing of all was that Mom still didn't seem to mind any of this. She wasn't angry with Dad or anything.

"I hope he gets a good breakfast at the hospital," she said, smiling. "He's so busy. He can use a good meal to start the day."

This was way too weird for me! I couldn't wait to get out of the house.

I ate a few more bites of oatmeal, then hurried off towards Taylor's home. We walked to class together every day.

I wasn't going to school today, though — not with Mr. Wicker planning to kill me. That was for sure.

I figured Taylor might skip school with me; together we could decide what to do about our crazy teacher.

The instant I walked into his living room, I told Taylor everything — all about Mr. Wicker and how he tried to kill me. I also told him about my parents and how they didn't even report Mr. Wicker's attack and all the rest of that stuff.

"Man, that is really strange," Taylor said. "It's so hard to imagine Mr. Wicker hurting someone. And you said your parents were acting even wackier this morning? I wonder what's wrong with them."

"I don't know but I wish they would get over it," I said. "I'm starting to feel like I'm in some old horror movie or something. Everyone's acting so bizarre. And now I think I'm getting a little sick from all of it, you know? My stomach hurts."

"Yeah, now that you mention it, Ben, you don't look too good. Your skin's kinda yellow. Maybe you should just go home and stay in bed."

"I can't lie around the house all day," I said. "Mr. Wicker might find me there. He might leave class and drive over and really kill me this time."

Suddenly, Taylor's eyes grew wide. He stared at me and his mouth fell open. Then he took two or three steps backwards, away from me.

"B-B . . . uh, Ben," he stammered, pointing at my face. "Your skin — something's happening. We gotta get you to a doctor or hospital or something!"

"Why? What's wrong?" I asked frantically, touching my face. My cheeks felt rough and scaly, like the face of a lizard or an alligator. "Taylor, what's happening?"

"I . . . I don't know, Ben! Go look in the mirror," he said. "See for yourself!"

I ran over to a mirror in his living room and peered at myself.

I was horrified at what I saw peering back at me! It was the ugliest face I'd ever seen!

There in the mirror was a kid who looked nothing like Benjamin Wackerman! I had small yellow scales covering my face! They were all over my skin, like a monster!

I looked like the creature from the slime lagoon!

Chapter Six

"*Aaaaaahhhh!*" I screamed.

"Ben, stay calm," Taylor said. "Stay calm, OK? We'll call your Dad, OK?"

"*Aaaaaahhhh!*"

"Stop looking in the mirror, Ben! Come on! Let's get you home, OK?" Taylor said. He grabbed my sleeve and tried to pull me away from the mirror.

It was the most ghastly sight I'd ever seen! It wasn't human!

But it was me!

That was my monster face in the mirror.

Why were all these terrible things happening to me?

First, Mr. Wicker had tried to murder me. Then my family had acted really weird when I told them about Mr. Wicker's attack. Then they had gotten even weirder at breakfast.

And now this. Horrible!

It was too much for a twelve-year-old kid to take!

As Taylor and I ran towards my house, I kept wondering if I'd done something to deserve this.

As someone who wants to be a scientist, I'm not usually superstitious. But facts are facts — and the facts were plain: extremely bad things were going on!

Was this stuff happening because I hadn't been doing my history homework? That seemed ridiculous. But Mr. Wicker always got angry with me during history class.

Using my powers of logic, I decided there had to be some connection between history lessons and the terrible trouble breaking out all around me.

But what? What did any of these things have to do with history?

So that couldn't be true. Or could it?

We ran up the steps to my house. I was huffing and puffing but I had stayed right behind Taylor the whole way, even though he was a lot stronger than me. I think my fear gave me extra strength.

As we hurried into my kitchen, I felt terrified. I

knew Taylor was scared, too, though he tried not to show it.

"OK, just sit down, Ben. I'll call your Dad to come home right away," Taylor said, panting.

"Help me, Taylor. I don't want to look like some freak from a monster movie the rest of my life," I pleaded. "I'll never get a girlfriend like this!"

"Try to relax, Ben. Your Dad's a big-time doctor. He'll know what to do," Taylor said, reaching for the telephone. "Now just tell me your Dad's number at work and . . . "

He was interrupted by a man's voice coming from the shadows of our kitchen. It was a deep, strange voice. A voice I hadn't heard before.

"You won't need that number, Taylor," the voice announced slowly. "I'm right here."

The man stepped out of the shadows.

He had a heavy black beard and long black hair. His clothes were all black, too. His eyes looked dark and angry.

He gazed at my friend and me like a hungry man staring at two T-bone steaks. Worst of all, he held a long knife in his right hand, ready to carve us into bite-sized bits.

I was so shocked I couldn't even scream. Neither could Taylor.

Some kind of kid-killer had slipped into my house after Mom left for work!

Slowly, step by step, he walked towards me, gradually raising the knife towards my throat!

Chapter Seven

The killer walked slowly, moving forward only a few inches with each step.

It was as if he was torturing me with fear, carrying his knife across the kitchen towards me in slow motion.

"*Noooo*! Don't kill me!" I begged.

"Leave us alone!" Taylor ordered. "Get out of this house now!"

Taylor was brave, and he was large and athletic. I could tell he was getting ready to pounce on the man.

Taylor had to know he would be risking his life. But he wasn't about to run away without doing all he could to stop this maniac.

He's really the best friend a guy could have.

I glanced at Taylor just as he was ready to leap. Suddenly his expression changed.

"D-Dr. Wackerman? Is . . . is that you?" Taylor asked.

I was stunned. Could this really be my father?

"Yes, Taylor," the killer replied. "It's me."

Chapter Eight

None of this made any sense.

It defied logic! It defied science! It defied nature!

My own father had left our house for work only an hour or so earlier, looking like himself. He was young and well dressed and handsome, though perhaps a little pudgy like me, I guess.

But now he had been transformed into a wacko with a knife!

At the same time, I had changed into something that resembled an alien in Star Wars!

"Dad, is that really you?" I asked, my voice quavering. "What happened to you, Dad? What's going on?"

"Benny? Is that you, boy?" Dad asked. "I thought I was losing my mind. I heard Taylor call you 'Ben' and your voice sounded like my son. But . . .

well, I thought you had to be someone else — someone horrible. Something has happened to you, too, Benny. Something awful is happening to our whole family."

"Where's Mom? She's not hurt, is she?"

"No, she's not exactly hurt, Benny. But she isn't well either, son. She's suffering from the same troubles as you and me," he answered.

With that, an old woman who looked nothing like my mother stepped into the kitchen.

"Hi Benny, dear," the woman said.

It was her voice. The voice of my mom. But this couldn't be my beautiful, young mother!

This woman looked a hundred and fifty years old!

Her hair wasn't just gray — it was yellow and falling out of her head. She had long gray hairs growing from her chin and nose in two or three places.

The lines in her face were so deep she looked like a human raisin!

It was as if someone had found the world's oldest woman and given her decaying body to my mother!

"No, Mom!" I cried. "It can't be you!"

"Benny, darling, I don't know what's wrong,

but some horrible disease is afflicting our family," Mom said, putting her old hands around my scaly face to comfort me. "Your father has no idea what's wrong. He's even talked to some special doctors from his hospital. They don't know either."

My mother started to cry.

"Yes, son," my dad said. "I'm doing everything I can. I've even talked to some colleagues at the Mayo Clinic. But no one has heard of anything like this."

As he spoke, his face turned even darker, right before our eyes. Jagged scars started to appear on his skin. His beard and hair grew longer.

Mom's back started hunching over, as if she was aging still more. Hunks of her yellow hair fluttered to the floor, leaving bald patches all over her scalp.

And my scaly skin began to come off my face in sheets. Skin peeled away like it does after a bad sunburn.

Underneath the outer layer my skin looked even scalier than before, bright green rather than yellow. I really was starting to look like some kind of reptile.

"We can't do anything to stop this!" Mom whimpered through her tears. "Oh, why is this happening?"

"There's got to be a logical reason for this," Dad replied. "Stay strong, dear. You too, Benny. I'll find some way to help us."

Dad didn't sound like he believed his own words, though.

"We're doomed," I said, starting to cry along with Mom. "This thing is just getting worse and worse. My whole family is going to die!"

Chapter Nine

Through all of this horror, Taylor stood silently.

I could tell that he was scared, really scared! Who wouldn't be? His best friend's family was being transformed into horrible, weird-looking creatures.

But I also could see that he was thinking about ways to end our misery.

"You can't just give up, Ben!" Taylor said suddenly. "I just know that somebody out there can tell us what to do about this problem!"

"But *who*?" I said. "No one on earth can do anything for us if the doctors don't know how to help! Dad doesn't have a clue what to do! We're doomed, I tell you! You should go home, Taylor, so you don't have to look at us! We're so ugly and we're going to die!"

But Taylor wouldn't leave. He stayed right by my side and even put his hand on my shoulder a couple times to help give me courage.

He asked me questions. Then he asked my dad and mom some more questions. He stopped to listen when Dad suggested ideas.

Then Taylor came up with an idea of his own — an idea that sounded totally nuts to me at first.

"I think I've got it!" he said. "Remember, Ben? My sister believes in supernatural stuff. I know you think Lynn's kinda weird, but she swears that psychics can see into another world where there's spooks and spirits and past lives and things. And she says some psychics can solve all kinds of problems."

"A *psychic*!" I shouted. "Are you going bananas or what?"

"Wait a minute, Benny. Let's think about this," Dad said. "We don't have a lot of choices now. Maybe Taylor's onto something."

"Yeah, Ben — I mean, I know you're like this smart science guy and everything. But sometimes even scientists can't explain everything," Taylor said. "What have we got to lose? Maybe Lynn knows what she's talking about. I think I should call her. I'll ask the name of the best psychic she knows."

And that's just what Taylor did.

I was still skeptical about anyone who claimed to possess supernatural powers. I mean, that's one thing science has done for the world, you know?

Science has helped make us less superstitious about dumb things, like black cats and witches and walking under ladders and nonsense of all sorts.

But here I was, Mr. Future Scientist, going to a psychic to ask for help. It seemed like a silly, desperate thing to do.

I was feeling pretty desperate, I guess.

So Taylor and I walked down the street towards this psychic's house, which was only about four blocks from mine. I was wearing a hat and thick scarf to help hide my scaly appearance.

But now and then, someone in the street caught a glimpse of my ugliness above my scarf — and hurried off in the other direction.

I must have looked terrifying to them. Imagine bumping into a person with thick green scales on his face.

I felt like a crocodile walking in winter clothes down the sidewalk.

Pretty soon we came to 4175 Oxblood Street, where the psychic lived. It was an old, dumpy-looking two-story house with rotting boards on the porch and peeling paint everywhere.

I laughed bitterly to myself about the paint. I thought, this place must look the way my face looks — gross and peeling like a moldy onion!

We rang the doorbell. It gonged once loudly, like a cathedral bell. The door squeaked as it opened and a woman stood there smiling.

She sure wasn't the sort of woman I expected to find in a rundown house like that.

This woman was beautiful!

She had long black hair and skin the color of milk chocolate and round, dark eyes. She was tall with long, slim legs and strong muscles all over her body. She looked like one of the best-looking women in the world to me.

She was wearing a short white robe that was draped over one shoulder. Her feet were bare.

"Hello, boys," she said in a soft voice, almost a whisper. "My name is Marlene. I was expecting you. Come in."

We walked through Marlene's parlor, which was loaded with black wooden sculptures and bright red and yellow paintings. Everything looked as if it was from Africa.

The scent of jasmine incense floated through the air. The faint sound of music floated from overhead, as if someone in an upstairs room were playing a violin.

It was dark and mysterious in the house, which was lit only by several candles.

We entered another room through a curtain of beads that clattered and clacked as we passed. I was sure Marlene would have a crystal ball or a deck of Tarot cards or a Ouija board.

You know, some fake-type thing to pretend to see into the spirit world.

But she didn't.

Instead, there was only a long couch and two old wooden chairs. Marlene sat on one of the chairs without a word.

Then she gestured towards the couch with a wave of her hand and Taylor and I sat down.

I was nervous and Taylor seemed nervous too as he fidgeted around on the couch. I still was wearing my hat and scarf to avoid frightening the psychic.

"I guess you're wondering why we're here, Marlene," Taylor began. "Well, it's kinda strange to explain but . . . "

Marlene held out her hand to silence Taylor.

"I know why you are here," she whispered. "And I can help you."

"Oh sure, you're a psychic. How stupid can I be? Of course you'd know," Taylor said. "See Ben, I told you she was supposed to be really good at this."

"No, you do not understand me," Marlene said. "I know why you have come only because your sister, Lynn, called to tell me about your trouble."

At least this psychic is honest, I thought. She could have pretended that her great powers had revealed everything before we even arrived.

But I still didn't trust this woman. Not at all.

No matter how beautiful she was.

Maybe Marlene was only trying to make us believe she was honest. Then she would fool us and demand a lot of money or something.

I knew from reading newspaper stories that most psychics are con artists.

Could Marlene really be any different?

"Take off your hat, Ben," Marlene said so softly I barely heard her. "Take off your hat and your scarf so that I can see the wicked thing that has taken hold of you."

Very slowly, I lifted the hat off my head, then unwound the long scarf from my neck and face. Then I looked at Marlene, dreading her expression of terror.

Marlene just gazed at me calmly, studying me like a map. She stood up and touched the hideous scales on my face, brushing them softly with her wrist.

Then she kissed the top of my head.

Gross!

How could she stand to do that?

Marlene moved her chair close to the couch, held our hands and closed her eyes.

The candlelight washed over her smooth skin and black shadows danced in the corners of the room. The violin music murmured over our heads.

Marlene said nothing. She seemed to be listening, her brow furrowed in concentration.

Feeling worried, I glanced at Taylor. What was this woman doing anyway?

For a long time, the psychic was silent. Then, at last, she spoke to us in a whisper.

"Ohhh, my child," she began softly. "My poor child!"

"Wh-what do you see?" I asked.

"I see troubles long, long past. I see blood and heartache and the sting of the whip. I see tears, oceans of tears. I see hatred and cruelty and it has not ended for you, my child," Marlene explained.

"But what are you talking about?" Taylor asked. "Can't you tell us what you mean?"

"And what to do about it?" I added, terrified.

"I can look into the depths of your family," Marlene went on, her eyes still closed. "But I see darkness and wickedness and ignorance for centuries. Many long centuries past. There is a curse upon you and your family, my child. A terrible curse. And this black stain will live for centuries more, destroying you and your parents and anyone in your family who is born after you."

She opened her eyes wide and stared straight at me.

"All of you," she said, "will die a horrible, painful death!"

Chapter Ten

Marlene closed her eyes again and sat still as ice, holding our hands.

She shivered, as if cold. But I think she was afraid.

The psychic was looking into my family's dark past — and our awful future!

"This curse on your family has lain asleep for more than one hundred years," she whispered. "But someone has come into your life and awakened it. Now the curse is alive again and turning you and your family into images of shame. Your father is growing mean. Your mother becomes old and decayed. And you resemble the reptiles of the foul swamps."

The candles flickered from a draft somewhere, making the shadows bend and sway.

Taylor and I glanced at each other, frozen with fear.

"But why?" I asked. "Why has this happened?"

Marlene closed her eyes even tighter and frowned.

"A horrible thing was done by your family, Ben," she answered slowly. "Long ago. A horrible thing for which your family now must suffer."

"B-but *we* didn't do it!" I protested. "Whatever it was, it wasn't me or Dad or Mom! Why should *we* have to pay for something some old guy did a hundred years ago?"

"You must pay for the sins of your family, my child. You are descended from a line of villains. There is nothing you can do to stop this vengeance on the Wackermans," Marlene said. "Except, perhaps, one thing."

"One thing? What?" Taylor demanded.

"Please, Marlene!" I added.

"If you can return to the scene of this evil, you may be able to change your fate," she said. "You must go back in time and destroy the one man in your family most responsible for this curse. You must put the past right again, Ben. Step back into history and undo the wrongs committed in your family's name."

"Back into history?" I asked.

"That's impossible!" Taylor said.

"Only if this is done will you and your family have a chance to live," the psychic continued. "You must find the crime and the man who first committed it. Then you must destroy him!"

"But how can we go back into history?" I exclaimed. "No one can do that — not even the best scientist in the world!"

"There is a way, my child. Only one way. And you must find it," Marlene replied. "You must discover the door to the past and step through it. Then you must destroy the man who is destroying your family!"

Chapter Eleven

Taylor and I walked down the street towards my house.

We were totally weirded out!

Travel back through time?

Marlene-the-psychic must be a fraud like all the rest of them, I thought angrily. But I had to admit that she had not asked us for any money.

She was up to something, though, that was for sure.

Undo past crimes? Find the villain? Go back in time?

As if!

Neither Taylor nor I said very much. We hung our heads as we trudged towards my home. We had nothing but bad news for my parents.

The Wackerman family really was doomed.

It didn't matter whether Marlene was telling the

truth or not. We didn't know how to go back in time.

That meant we were all going to die — probably soon.

Suddenly, though, Taylor stopped in his tracks and snapped his fingers. Then he looked at me and, for the first time that day, a slight smile spread across his face. I wondered what could be making him happy when we were in a mess like this.

"Wait, Ben!" he said, and I heard excitement in his voice. "My sister has this book I was reading one night. It's some book that's so old it's falling apart. But Lynn left it in the bathroom and I was stuck sitting in there because I'd eaten beans and — well anyway, I remember something I read in that book."

We walked by a store as we talked, and I caught a glimpse of my reflection in the window.

"I hope this book can help," I said. "From the looks of it, I'd say we don't have any time to waste. I'm getting worse every minute."

"Your scales are getting thicker and greener, Ben. And your parents must be getting worse too," Taylor said, starting to run down the sidewalk. "Come on! We've got to hurry!"

Taylor ran towards his house as fast as he could and I tried to keep up with him. This time, though, I couldn't do it. I was puffing so hard I thought I was going to drop dead right on the pavement.

I think I was getting weaker from the curse. My stomach was starting to hurt again and I had no energy. I just wanted to go to sleep.

But I kept running anyway. My parents' lives were at stake.

And so was mine.

When I finally opened the door to Taylor's house, I found him sitting in the living room with the old book already in his lap. He was flipping through the worn pages like a madman.

"It's got to be here somewhere!" he said. "I know I saw that thing about time travel."

"What did you say?" I asked, breathing almost too hard to talk. "Time travel? In that book?"

"Yeah, that's what I read in here. Come on, where is it?" he replied, still turning pages furiously. "Ah! Here it is!"

"You really found it? Time travel?"

"Yeah, right here. I'll read it to you," Taylor

said. "But you'd better sit down, Ben. You look like you're going to pass out."

I sat beside him, still trying to catch my breath.

Taylor placed his hands carefully around the cover of the old book. It looked dusty and stained with age. The pages were yellowing, and many of them were so loose they were almost falling out.

The title was still faintly visible across the cover. It said: "Potions of Medieval Science." I could also read that the book had been published in Boston in 1855.

Taylor cleared his throat and began to read:

"You must recall, dear reader, that science has come far from the days of the medieval men who practiced it. Yet, as we have seen in earlier chapters, some of their discoveries seem remarkable to us — even today, in the mid-19th Century.

"However, one of the most interesting discoveries has long been dismissed as a potion without any power. Modern scientists scoff at the claim that a mixture of simple substances can send a man back into time. If only it were true!

"How many of us would volunteer for that

journey! Still, we include the formula in this volume for its value as a curiosity. It is worth nothing more than a passing glance today."

I sighed wearily, peeling off another layer of green scales from my face.

"Even back a hundred and fifty years ago they knew this formula couldn't work," I said. "It's hopeless, Taylor."

"Ben, your face is getting a lot worse," Taylor said. "I can see how weak you are. This is our only chance to save you and your family. Just listen, OK?"

"This formula was developed by a king's sorcerer in the year 1245. But the sorcerer was really a serious man of science," he read.

"Fearing that his king might misuse the potion, the sorcerer recorded the formula for future generations — then buried his notes in a wooden cask in the castle graveyard. In one note, the sorcerer explained his potion's great secret: It allows anyone who mixes these chemicals in their precise amounts to go back into time.

"He also claimed that the formula permits the time traveler to change into the shape of anyone who was alive during any period of history. All the time traveler must do is imagine the person he wants to be.

"He then will become that person instantly — but only in appearance and voice. No matter whom the traveler resembles, his mind and previous experiences always remain the same.

"Finally, the sorcerer also included a simple formula for the antidote — the potion to wipe away the spell and bring the traveler back to his own time. Without that antidote, anyone who journeys back into the past will be lost forever."

Taylor stopped reading and looked up.

"Wow," he said. "Pretty cool."

"Like the book says, it would be cool if it were true," I replied. "But it can't be. It just can't! Though I wish it were. My skin is peeling off so fast I'll be nothing but bones soon. I'm feeling weaker every second. I think I might be dying, Taylor."

"Then we've got to try this formula, Ben! We've *got* to!" Taylor said. "I remember Mr. Wicker once told us in class that good scientists admit how much they don't know. We can't explain everything — even with science. Maybe this medieval formula works."

I was fading quickly. I had no energy to argue.

So I agreed to try the formula. I prayed that it might really allow us to travel back into the past.

Was it possible? Could Taylor and I fly back through time and fix the evil done by my ancestors?

It seemed the last dim hope for the survival of the Wackerman family.

And it looked to me like a very slim hope indeed.

Chapter Twelve

Taylor was running wildly around his house.

I could hear him talking to himself as he gathered the ingredients listed in the formula.

"OK, OK — that's the salt. Now, thyme. Right, Mom has thyme. Here it is," he said. Then he called out to me. "I think we have all this stuff right in the house, Ben! It's all pretty basic, mostly cooking stuff. Hang in there!"

He raced upstairs into his bathroom for something, then charged back into the living room where I was sitting.

"OK, Ben. Here it is. It's everything — all here," he said. "I'll read the formula to you and you mix the stuff in this jar my mom uses for leftover soup."

"I can't do it, Taylor. I can't move," I said miserably. "I'm too weak. You'd better mix it."

"No, no! You have to do it! You're the chemistry expert. And the book says these chemicals have to be measured precisely. I'll just mess it up," Taylor said. "You've got to find the strength to do this, Ben. Your mom and dad are probably dying right now. This is their only chance!"

His reminder about my parents helped give me extra strength. I imagined them at home, feeling weak, looking ghastly — and dying, like me. They needed me to save them!

I struggled from the chair onto the floor, where Taylor sat with the chemicals and measuring spoons.

One by one, I began to mix the chemicals together, concocting the ancient formula.

"It says a pinch of salt," Taylor said. "Is there a spoon to measure that? Do you know how much they mean by a pinch?"

"Yes," I answered weakly, squeezing the tiniest amount of salt between my thumb and forefinger. "This is a pinch."

"And a dash of sage. Here's the sage. But what's a dash?"

"Here," I responded, taking the can and sprinkling a bit of sage into the jar.

After the final ingredient was added — ten drops of vinegar — I mixed them all together with a wooden spoon, just as the instructions told us to do.

Taylor and I looked at the jar with disgust. The formula looked like really gross green soup.

Yuck!

"Well, I guess we'd better drink some, huh?" Taylor said at last.

"Yes," I said. "I don't have much energy left, Taylor. I won't last much longer. I'll try it first and hope it works."

My friend handed me the jar and I raised it to my lips. But before I could take a sip, Taylor grabbed my hand.

"No! Don't!" he screamed.

"What's wrong? I can't wait any longer, Taylor. I'm dying."

"But the antidote — remember? We have to make that too! If we don't take that with us, we'll be lost in the past forever," he said. "We'll never be able to get back!"

But I knew I didn't have time to wait for the antidote.

I didn't have time for anything any more.

I was dying — fast!

And Taylor could see it happening before his eyes.

We both understood that I only had two choices left. Neither was a good one.

I could either wait for Taylor to mix the antidote — and almost certainly die before he was done.

Or I could drink the formula I had made, which might send me zooming off into history with no way to ever get back home!

Chapter Thirteen

"I've gotta drink this," I said weakly. "I . . . I just gotta. *Please*, Taylor! Let me drink!"

Taylor was frantic. He didn't know what to do.

Should he keep me from drinking the only thing on earth that might save my life? Or should he let me travel back in time and be lost forever?

He looked at me. Then he looked at the jar that held the gross green gunk that could save me.

Then he looked at me again. Then he looked at the jar.

At me. At the jar.

Me. The jar.

I could see panic in Taylor's eyes.

What should he do? What would *you* do?

There were only two choices and both were wrong!

Or were there only two?

Taylor was scrunching his forehead, deep in thought. He was smart enough to know that there are almost always more than two choices. I could see that he was desperately trying to think of the third and fourth choices.

Just as I was ready to take my final breath of life, Taylor snapped his fingers.

"I know! *Yessss!*" he shouted. "Here Ben, drink it! Drink half of it right now!"

Taylor held the jar of green goop to my lips. Slowly, he poured half the liquid down my throat.

It tasted as gross as it looked.

But I slurped and gurgled and swallowed as fast as I could. Then I closed my eyes, exhausted.

And I waited. I wondered what would happen next.

Then I heard Taylor swallowing the rest of the gunk.

He lay on the floor beside me and placed his hand gently on my shoulder.

"Hang on, Ben! Hang in there, pal!" he pleaded. "This is gonna work for us! I know it is!"

"Taylor . . . we'll be . . . lost forev . . . lost forever," I whispered as I lay near death.

"No, Ben. No! We'll make it back home again," my buddy promised. "I'm going with you, Ben. I drank the potion. I have a plan to get us back home. I'm pretty sure — I mean, my plan *should* work. Uh, I hope."

Chapter Fourteen

Without warning, I felt like I was spinning around in a swivel chair.

And spinning really fast!

I mean, spinning faster than anyone could possibly spin — you know, like a thousand times a second. Around and around and around.

Everything looked blurry. But I wasn't dizzy.

And something else was really weird: I felt like somebody had one finger stuck up my nose!

I know it sounds funny but it's true.

I wondered if I was dying. Maybe this is what happens when you die, I thought.

Maybe God puts you in a swivel chair and spins you around really fast with his finger up your nose!

Hey, it's possible, I guess. As a future scientist, I had trained myself to believe in the facts I observed.

And these strange feelings were major facts —

facts I could feel myself.

I wasn't really scared. Just kind of tense, like I was waiting for something important to happen to me.

As I kept spinning and spinning and spinning, I heard a woman's voice whisper to me. She sounded a little like Marlene, the psychic woman Taylor and I had visited.

"Choose," the voice breathed.

That was all. Just this single word, whispered only once: "Choose!"

For some reason, in the next moment I thought of Abraham Lincoln. I have no idea why.

But that's the one thought that popped into my head.

Abraham Lincoln — probably the greatest U.S. president ever. The man who kept the United States together during the Civil War.

Somehow, I could see him standing in front of me. I could see his thin face and dark beard, his long arms and legs.

In the next instant, I was standing alone inside a beautiful room. I didn't know where I was. But I wasn't dead, that's for sure.

I wasn't spinning anymore. No one had a finger up my nose, either.

Also, I didn't feel weak or sick any longer.

I couldn't wait to find out what I looked like now. Was my face still full of green scales, all ugly and gruesome?

I looked around the room for a mirror. I didn't see one, but I noticed that this was a very unusual room.

It was shaped kind of like an oval, but not quite. There was a big brown wooden desk at one end, sitting in front of three huge windows.

Behind the desk stood an American flag. But it didn't look exactly like the ones I always saw at school and the post office. It was different, though I didn't know how.

Whatever, I thought.

But I kept thinking, I wonder where I am? And what do I look like now?

Why don't I feel like I'm dying anymore?

Where's Taylor? He had a plan to get back home from time travel. Without him, I was lost in history forever!

And how are Mom and Dad?

I prayed they were both still alive!

I still felt confused about everything. Maybe if I look out the window, I thought, I can figure out where I am.

"Man, this whole thing is really, really weird," I said out loud.

Then things got weirder! Because my voice didn't sound like me!

It was the voice of a full-grown man, kind of a high-pitched voice with an accent of some kind. I said something else just to hear it again.

"This is Ben Wackerman talking. Hey! This sure doesn't sound like Ben Wackerman," I said.

I couldn't believe my ears.

Now I was incredibly curious, and pretty frightened too. Where was I anyway?

And what had happened to my voice?

I walked over to the tall set of three windows and looked outside.

I could see a huge lawn, maybe the biggest lawn I'd ever seen. There were lots of trees and stuff all around the grass.

And there were a lot of small buildings across the street. For some reason, a couple of guys were riding by in carriages pulled by horses. Maybe this was a theme park, I thought, like Disney World.

Then I saw the strangest thing of all.

So strange that it made me gasp in shock. I noticed my own reflection in the glass window.

But the face looking back at me wasn't mine.

It was the face of Abraham Lincoln!

Chapter Fifteen

Impossible!

That's the first thing I thought.

I was seeing this with my own eyes. But I s
didn't believe it.

I brought my face so close to the glass that my nose touched the window. Then I backed up a little.

Then I moved my head to the right and to the left. Each time, the face of Abe Lincoln moved with me.

I really had gone back in time after all! And I had morphed into the great man. I was now the President of the United States during the Civil War.

Words can't explain how surprised I was. Surprised — and badly spooked.

I screamed as loud as I had ever screamed in my life!

"*Aaaahhhhhhh!*" I yelled. "*Aaaahhhhhhh!*"

A white door opened immediately and a woman stepped inside the office. She was holding a pencil and I understood that she was probably Lincoln's secretary.

"Are you all right, sir?" she asked. "I heard you cry out."

"Me? Oh, uh — well, yes. Oh, sure. I feel awesome," I answered nervously in Lincoln's high voice.

"Awesome, sir?" my secretary asked. "I'm not quite certain I follow your meaning, Mr. President."

"Oh — uh, yes," I said.

I remembered that I was in a different time now. The people who lived during the 1860s didn't talk like kids do today!

"Pardon me, ma'am," I said. "Yes, I'm fine. I, uh — well, the truth is that I just pinched my finger in this desk drawer."

She looked at me as if I'd lost my mind.

"All right, Mr. President. Let me know if you need anything," she said, starting to close the door.

Then she poked her head back inside.

"Mr. President, did you call me 'ma'am?'" she asked. "You've never called me that before. It was so odd that I wondered if I'd done anything wrong, sir?"

"Uh, no, of course not," I said awkwardly. "No, just hurt my finger a bit, that's all. No harm done. Uh, Miss — I mean, uh, Mrs. — um . . . "

"Kennedy, sir. You always just call me Mrs. Kennedy. Remember, Mr. President?" she said, looking worried. "I'll be just outside the Oval Office if you want me, sir."

"Yes, Mrs. Kennedy. That's fine. Just fine," I responded with a weak smile.

Mrs. Kennedy closed the door. I walked to Lincoln's desk and sat down.

I was relieved that my — uh, I mean President Lincoln's — secretary had left. But I didn't know what to do.

I had no clue at all. I sure understood, though, that this time travel thing was going to be hard.

Really hard.

That's when I thought about the friend who was supposed to have traveled in time with me. What about Taylor, I wondered.

What had happened to my best friend — the guy who had saved my life by giving me the green gunk to drink?

At that moment, I heard heavy footsteps outside the office. Then I heard a man's deep voice booming as he talked to Mrs. Kennedy.

Soon there was a knock at my office door.

"Come in," I answered, trying to talk with the confidence of a president.

"Excuse me, Mr. President. But General Grant wants to see you," Mrs. Kennedy said.

Uh-oh! This could be big trouble!

General Grant was the top officer for the United States in the war against the Confederates. He was the commander of the entire Union army.

Now he wanted to talk business — with *me*. Me, President Lincoln.

What did I know about fighting a war? Nothing, that's what.

I didn't even know anything about the Civil War because I hated history lessons so much. I rarely read my history book.

What was I going to do now?

Whatever it was, I had to do it fast.

"Yeah, OK — I mean, yes. Well, I am a bit busy right now. Perhaps he could come back a bit later, Mrs.

Kennedy," I suggested.

She again looked at me as if I had said something strange.

"But Mr. President," she said, "you asked that General Grant come to the White House, sir. He's traveled all the way from Virginia to meet with you today — at your request. But if you like, I'll ask the general to come back later, sir."

"Um, well, of course not. Yes, I did send for him, didn't I?" I replied with an uncomfortable cough. "Yes, Mrs. Kennedy. Yes, yes — of course, send General Grant in."

This should be interesting, I thought. Just wait until General Grant finds out that President Lincoln can't remember anything about the Civil War!

The door opened again and a large, strong-looking man with a brown beard stepped in. He was wearing a Union general's uniform that still had mud on it from the last battle.

His boots were muddy, too. They left clumps of dirt wherever he walked.

I recognized him immediately. Anyone would know him, even if they had never opened a history book.

It really was General Ulysses S. Grant.

"Mr. President," he said, smiling and extending his hand. "It's good to see you again, sir."

"General, I'm mighty happy to see you too," I answered, hoping President Lincoln said things like "mighty happy."

All of a sudden, General Grant got a strange expression on his face. He glanced over both his shoulders, making sure no one was in the office with us. Then he looked at me and smiled.

"Well, thank you, Mr. President. Yes, we surely need to talk about this war, don't we? Except uh, Mr. President — can I ask you a question, sir? I know it may sound a bit unusual," General Grant said. "Um, Mr. President, I was wondering if you knew the chemical symbol for water, sir?"

I almost choked.

This was a bizarre question for a general to ask his president. Especially in the White House during Civil War days.

What was going on here?

I tried to calm down and answer him as if such

questions were common in the White House. I would play along and find out what he was up to.

"Of course I can tell you, General," I quickly replied. "The symbol is H_2O. Why do you ask me, sir, if I may inquire?"

General Grant looked over both shoulders again. Then he leaned towards me and whispered.

I couldn't have been more stunned by his next words.

"Ben?" General Grant asked. "Is that you? It's me — Taylor!"

Chapter Sixteen

For a moment, everything confused me. I couldn't put this century together with the one I came from.

I didn't know how to respond to this famous 19th-century general who said he was a friend from the 20th.

"Uh, I'm not quite sure of your intentions here, sir," I said.

That was the best I could do under these confusing circumstances. What if it wasn't really Taylor?

"Ben. That's got to be you in there," General Grant said. "It's really me, Taylor! Tell me this is you, Ben! I asked you about the chemical symbol for water you — I mean Ben Wackerman — knows that. And I didn't think President Lincoln would."

I smiled with relief and shook his hand. It was really Taylor after all!

"Yeah, Taylor. It's me!" I said. "I wasn't sure if you might be pretending to be my friend. Who knows what can happen in time travel? Maybe you were just testing me."

"Well, I'm really Taylor even though I look like General Grant," he said. "This whole thing really is a mind-bender, isn't it? I can't believe that I'm suddenly this big general walking around Washington."

"I know what you mean," I said. "You should try being President Lincoln! My secretary thinks I'm nuts! I didn't even know her name," I said. "But Taylor, I've got to ask you something. Do you really have some plan to get us both home again? Or are we stuck in time travel forever?"

"Sure, Ben, I've really got a plan," Taylor said. "Before I drank the green gunk, I ripped the page with the antidote formula from my sister's book. See, here it is. If we can find the right ingredients, you can mix them together and we'll get home to the present."

"Just don't lose that page," I said. "Without that, we're goners."

"It's here, safe inside my pocket," Taylor said. "But I don't think we should stay around the White

House too long, Ben. Somebody is going to get suspicious of us real fast. If they ask a simple question, like the name of Lincoln's wife, we'll be in trouble when we don't know."

"It was Mary Todd Lincoln," I said. "But I agree with you. We should leave here — except I don't know what we're supposed to do. Marlene told us we had to find the guy in my family who had done all that bad stuff."

"And destroy him," Taylor said. "I don't know why we ended up here, in the middle of the Civil War. But maybe it means this guy was alive during this period of history."

"I think you might be right," I said. "Remember, we were doing a history lesson on the Civil War just before Mr. Wicker tried to strangle me? And when I was traveling in time, spinning around like crazy, I thought about President Lincoln. I'm not sure why. But that's when I morphed into him. There has to be a reason we landed in the 1860s."

After discussing the situation, Taylor and I came up with an idea. We decided that we should go to the front lines of the Civil War.

Then we would talk to some of the other generals — the *real* Union generals.

Maybe one of them had heard the name Wackerman before. If we were really lucky, one of those generals might know something about this bad guy from my family and give us a clue where to find him.

General Grant — I mean Taylor — and I rode with a couple of Union soldiers to the front lines in Virginia, sitting in a horse-drawn carriage. My friend tried his best to act like a tough general in the U.S. Army.

"Soldier, pull the horses up over there," he ordered at one point. "Yes, by that forest there. The president needs to stop for the bathroom and wants to use one of those trees."

I laughed when Taylor said that. But I really did have to go, and I figured he was right. Even presidents probably used trees for bathrooms back in the Civil War.

Of course, I also tried hard to play the part of President Lincoln — the worried man in charge of Grant and all the armies of the Union.

I asked some questions loud enough so the soldiers driving the carriage could hear me.

"General, do you think this war is going to last much longer?" I asked. "I hate to see any more of our boys get killed."

"President Lincoln, I plan to break the back of the Rebel army soon," the fake Grant replied. "And we'll have all our soldiers home before Easter."

When we finally arrived at the huge Union camp, thousands of men dressed in blue uniforms marched through the mud around us. They looked dirty and tired, and some of them seemed thirsty and hungry, too.

It didn't look like much fun to be a soldier.

I asked a sergeant where the other generals were staying. The sergeant escorted Taylor and me to a large tent. He told us the generals all were inside, planning tomorrow's battle.

Now, Taylor and I had another problem. Neither of us knew much about the Civil War. We couldn't call even the other officers by name. All we could do was try to bluff our way through, calling everyone "general."

Right then, I wished I had studied my history

lessons! Maybe I would at least have known the top generals of the Union army!

We walked inside the tent. All the generals stood up, saluting us. We saluted back and chatted pleasantly a few moments.

Then I asked each of them whether they had heard of anyone named Wackerman.

"No, Mr. President," the commanders replied one by one. "That name means nothing to me at all."

The pretend General Grant and I sat on dirty wooden chairs, listening to Union commanders explain their ideas for crushing the Confederate army of General Robert E. Lee.

Lee was the leader of all the Rebel troops, of course.

Taylor and I mostly just nodded and agreed with their battle plans — and hoped their suggestions were right.

And I worried. If the United States loses the Civil War because of me, I thought, my family will *never* get rid of that curse.

All this time, Taylor and I listened for any hints that might help us solve the mystery of the evil Wackerman family member.

The generals discussed which army divisions to march forward. They debated how many cannons to bring into battle. They argued about where the Union soldiers should attack first.

But Taylor and I heard nothing that helped our search for the baddest Wackerman who ever lived.

Suddenly, the tent flap opened and two soldiers entered, saluting Taylor and me — you know, President Lincoln and General Grant.

Taylor returned the salute and asked what they wanted. I sat calmly like a president, waiting for their explanations.

"Pardon us for intrudin', sirs," one soldier said nervously. "But Major Donald Melvin has just captured a Rebel spy. The major thought you would want to be informed."

"A spy in our camp?" the fake General Grant asked. "Who was he spying on, soldier?"

"Major Melvin said the prisoner was spyin' on President Lincoln, sir," the soldier said. "He was part of a plot to kill the president, sir. He and some other Rebs were plannin' to shoot President Lincoln in the head."

That's when I remembered that Abraham Lincoln had been assassinated — shot to death while watching a play with his wife. Was I going to be assassinated too?

Me, pudgy little Ben Wackerman, murdered just because I looked like Lincoln?

"Bring in the prisoner, soldier," I ordered in my best presidential voice. "I want to see this man who hoped to put a bullet in me."

Both soldiers saluted me, stepped outside the tent a moment, then returned, holding the Confederate spy between them.

My eyes almost bugged out of my head. My mouth fell open and I glanced at Taylor, who looked as shocked as me.

The spy was very tall and very skinny, with thin black hair greased straight back. He had a tiny mustache and a stubby, crooked nose and his pants were too short. And his clothes were all black.

Taylor and I recognized him instantly.

The rebel spy was our history teacher!

Mr. Wicker had gone back in time too — and he was trying to kill President Lincoln!

Chapter Seventeen

Or was Mr. Wicker really trying to kill *me*?

Maybe this pretend Rebel spy was just trying to kill the pretend President Lincoln!

I gulped in terror at the sight of the man!

His beady dark eyes latched onto me instantly. Those eyes were filled with the same wicked look of hate I had seen so many times during history class.

Even here, far back in the past, I couldn't escape Mr. Wicker!

I struggled to quiet down my emotions, to appear like I was the real Mr. Lincoln.

"I'd like to interrogate the prisoner. Release his arms," I said, stepping in front of Mr. Wicker. "So this is the man who wanted to kill me. What is your name, sir?"

"Parker Adderson Bierce is the name I go by, though this is not my real name," the spy responded. "I suppose my real name doesn't matter now. I assume that I will be executed at daylight tomorrow."

"Why should you assume that, sir?" I asked. "We have not mentioned your death."

"Because it is the custom, I believe, for people who fail at my trade," the spy said. "As this is so, there is little use concealing my real name. It is Horace Phinias Wackerman."

I could hardly hide my astonishment! Mr. Wicker said his name was really Wackerman!

It seemed crazy!

Was this spy really just someone who looked exactly like Mr. Wicker? Someone whose name was the same as mine?

Or was this really Mr. Wicker, after all? Had he traveled back in time, and was he now pretending his name was Wackerman just to spook me?

I was so frightened that I felt dizzy. I acted like nothing was wrong, though. I had to find out more about this man — and I couldn't let my fear show.

But Taylor was overcome by nervous coughing when he heard the spy say his name was Wackerman. My friend seemed so shaken up that I was afraid he might give us away.

"Control yourself, General Grant! I shall handle this," I said. Then I turned to the prisoner again. "Wackerman, you say? This is curious indeed. Only an hour or two earlier, General Grant and I were inquiring about you, sir. It is good timing on your part to appear before us this way. We won't have to search for you now."

"But I am sorry to appear before you without my stolen Union uniform. Your soldiers made me take it off and put on my own clothes when I was captured," Horace Wackerman replied. "I would much rather have crept up behind you in my blue uniform so that you suspected nothing. Then I would have fired a pistol at your head, sir."

I was beginning to believe this really wasn't Mr. Wicker after all. He sounded like a real Rebel.

"Why should you want to kill me? I am not a soldier," I said.

"No, but you are in charge of all the Union soldiers. And I am a gentleman of South Carolina," he explained. "My family has been slave owners for centuries, Mr. Lincoln. And you have tried to free the slaves!

I cannot allow this, sir. The Wackerman family traces its slave-owning roots back to the days of the Roman Empire. We have built our reputations and our fortunes on the backs of the men, women and children we have purchased! They are our *property*, sir!"

"But that is wrong, Mr. Wackerman! Can't you see that?" I said. "People should not own other people. All people should be allowed the freedom to live their lives as they choose."

"If that is so, then I assume that I am free to go," the slave owner Wackerman said with a smile. "I choose to return to my home and my family in South Carolina, Mr. Lincoln. If you are true to your beliefs, release me."

"You are not without wit, sir. But I shall leave your fate to my generals, who are better equipped to decide these things."

The pretend General Grant said nothing. But all the others said at once that the spy must die — and not in the morning, but now!

"Take him out and shoot him immediately!" one of the other generals ordered.

I was about to change that order, explaining

that I wanted to question the prisoner some more. The truth was that I needed to find out everything this Wackerman knew about his family's past — and to make sure that he wasn't really Mr. Wicker.

But I had no time to say anything.

Suddenly Horace Wackerman sprang forward like a cat, grabbing the pole that supported the tent.

The tent collapsed heavily around us. I could hear shouting and scuffling and orders from furious generals.

"Seize the prisoner!" they yelled. "Don't let him get away! Someone get us out of here! Take hold of that spy Wackerman and shoot him!"

Soon a group of soldiers lifted up the canvas. All of us climbed out from under it, brushing off dirt and mud from our clothes.

"Where is the prisoner?" Taylor asked one soldier. "That Wackerman fellow — he surely didn't get away! Did you capture him?"

"No sir, we didn't, General Grant, sir," the frightened soldier responded. "I am sorry to report to you, General, that the Rebel spy got clean away and escaped into the woods, sir! And now there ain't no sight of that rascal nowhere, sir!"

Chapter Eighteen

Taylor and I stood alone in the woods beyond the Union generals' tent.

Of course, we still looked and sounded just like Abraham Lincoln and General Grant, so everyone left us alone.

They thought Lincoln and Grant were planning some important war strategy or something.

But we weren't. Taylor and I were trying to decide what we had to do next to save my family.

We had just met a Southern slave owner from Civil War days — and his name was Wackerman, my family name.

But this slave owner looked exactly like my teacher, Mr. Wicker.

That coincidence seemed very bizarre. It made no sense.

After lots of discussion, Taylor and I decided

this spy wasn't our teacher. We felt sure he really was a Southern spy and slave owner.

And if we were right about that, then we finally had some good information to help us track down the worst Wackerman of all — the man we had to find to end the terrible curse.

"I think we should travel through time again," I insisted. "This spy just told us that the Wackermans family has roots going back to ancient Rome. And the Wackermans were slave owners all those years. So they must all have been pretty bad if they owned slaves, right? Maybe if we go back to Roman times, we can find the Wackerman who first started being so bad. I think he must be the guy we're looking for, Taylor! The original evil wacko Wackerman is in ancient Rome!"

"Maybe, Ben," my friend said, looking worried. "But where will we look when we get back in those Roman times? This Wackerman could live anywhere in the Roman Empire — or maybe even outside it."

"All we know is that the first Wackerman who owned slaves had to be some rich, powerful guy in the Roman Empire, right?" I said. "That means he probably lived in Rome. So we'll go back in time to the center of the Roman Empire — to Rome itself!"

"Wow," Taylor said. "We're going to ancient Rome! Who do you wanna be?"

"I think I should go back as Julius Caesar, the great Roman Emperor," I said. "That way I can ask lots of questions and everyone will try to help me because I'm their leader."

"Awesome! So can I be like — oh, what was that other guy's name who helped Caesar? Anthony somebody?"

"Marc Antony. Yeah, he was Caesar's best friend, a soldier and everything," I recalled, surprised by how much history I had actually learned in school. "You be Antony and I'll be Caesar, OK? That should work for us. But how do we do this, Taylor — you know, go back in time again?"

"My sister's book said we can be anyone we want," Taylor said. "All we have to do is imagine that we're the person. So I guess you should think of yourself as Julius Caesar and you'll morph into him."

"Yeah, and you think of yourself as Marc Antony," I said, looking around to make sure no Union soldiers were watching us. I didn't want some horrified private to watch Lincoln and Grant disappear before his eyes! "OK, then, let's do it, Taylor! Here we go, heading into history again, going backwards in time something like two thousand years!"

I closed my eyes and started to chant out loud: "I'm Julius Caesar, I'm Julius Caesar, I'm Julius Caesar."

Beside me, I heard Taylor speaking in the voice of General Grant: "And I'm Marc Antony, I'm Marc Antony, I'm Marc Antony."

In an instant, I felt like I was spinning around in a swivel chair again. Spinning really fast, just like before.

Everything looked blurry.

Then the same weird thing happened again: I felt like someone had a finger up my nose!

I kept spinning and spinning and spinning, then I heard that woman's voice whispering to me. Remember? The voice that sounded just like Marlene, the beautiful psychic.

The voice said quietly, "Choose."

I was still thinking of Julius Caesar when suddenly I found myself standing among tall marble columns. The floor was made of marble, too — highly polished and glossy.

I was wearing leather sandals and this white robe kind of thing — I think they call it a toga. And I felt something heavy on top of my head.

When I lifted it off, I found that it was a golden crown embedded with diamonds and rubies and emeralds.

I guess I really am Julius Caesar now, I thought with a smile. I had morphed into another great political leader more quickly than I could have brushed my teeth.

I didn't feel so scared going back in history this time.

I just wanted to find Marc Antony — uh, I mean Taylor — and then hunt down the Wackerman who was a big-time slave owner in Rome.

Then somehow destroy him!

I heard footsteps and a Roman soldier entered the hall. He wore a helmet and carried a shield and sword. I decided he was probably one of my guards.

"My lord, you have a visitor!" he said, saluting me by putting his right fist to his chest. "Marc Antony is here, as you ordered. Shall I bring him in?"

Amazing how this time travel thing worked, wasn't it? It seemed like my best friend was always coming to see me right after I arrived.

Maybe it was because we traveled through history together and Taylor always landed somewhere near me, I thought. Or maybe Marlene had helped us to get together.

I didn't have a clue.

However it had happened, I was glad to hear that "Marc Antony" was on his way to me.

The great Roman warrior's entrance into the hall was announced with a flourish of long gold trumpets.

"Marc Antony!" a guard said after the trumpets fell silent.

Taylor looked just the way I imagined Antony would look — short and powerful, with curly black hair. But he wasn't smiling.

I knew by my friend's expression that something was seriously wrong.

"Hail Caesar!" the fake Marc Antony said, saluting me with his right fist.

95

His voice sounded deep and adult, just like mine. Somehow we were speaking in Italian, though neither of us knew that language.

The strangest things kept happening as we went back into history! Things that no scientist in the world could explain — not even scientists living in 1999!

"Antony, welcome!" I said. "Do you have news for me?"

"I do, my lord. But I must speak to Caesar in private," he noted, glancing around the marble hall.

"Leave us!" I ordered the guards who had escorted Taylor into the hall. "I shall call if I need you!"

I almost laughed at the way I was giving so many orders. But, hey, I was like an actor playing a part.

And I knew if I messed this part up, someone might discover that Taylor and I were fakes. Then we were dead meat, for sure!

The hall was empty now except for Marc Antony and me.

"Taylor?" I whispered, looking at this unfamiliar face. "That's you, right?"

"Ben? Is that you in there?" he asked. "Wow,

you look just like Julius Caesar! Major cool! But Ben, I really do have news. Some of the news is good — but some of it's bad. Like, real bad!"

"We don't need more bad news," I said. "Not now, just when we're closing in on the most evil guy in my family. Tell me the good news first, OK?"

"Well, the good news is that I know how to find this Wackerman guy we're looking for," Taylor said. "I asked one of your guards if there was any record of slave owners here in Rome. He said every man wealthy enough to own slaves must pay lots of taxes. The names and addresses of all slave owners are written down in stone tablets at the Roman Hall of Records."

"Man, that's great! So all we have to do is go there and ask for the address of Wackerman! No problem!" I exclaimed. "But what's the bad news, Taylor?"

"The bad news is that I lost the sheet of paper with the antidote formula on it," he said, his lip quivering. "We have no way to get back home, Ben! It's my fault and I'm really, really sorry! The formula was in my pants pocket when I was General Grant but somehow it fell out. We're stuck traveling in the past for good — lost in time forever and ever!"

Chapter Nineteen

I laughed.

I laughed so hard that I felt sure I was going to fall down and roll around the floor.

I laughed so hard that I thought the Roman guards would hear me and think Caesar had gone nutso!

Taylor thought I was losing my marbles for sure.

"Ben? Calm down! I'm sorry I lost the formula," he pleaded. "Just stop being hysterical, OK?"

"I — I'm not hy-hysterical, Taylor," I said, trying to stop laughing. "It's just that I'm so relieved! We're not lost in time! *I've* got the antidote formula. See, it's right here."

I pulled a piece of folded paper from under the belt of my toga. Taylor looked at it — then he started laughing too.

"You have it! You have it!" he shouted happily in his deep Italian voice. "Ben, it's a miracle! We're saved! How did you find it?"

"I picked it up in the Union camp after that spy pulled the tent down on us," I said. "It must have fallen out of your pocket during the struggle. I found it in the mud and slipped it into my pocket. But we got so busy talking about what to do that I forgot to tell you. Sorry, Taylor."

"I'm just glad it's not lost," my friend said. "Man, that was scary! But come on, let's go to the Hall of Records, OK? The sooner we get there, the sooner we can find this Wackerman guy and get back home to our parents."

Accompanied by Roman guards, Taylor and I — the pretend Marc Antony and the pretend Julius Caesar — rode in chariots to the Hall of Records.

We walked inside together, waving as Roman workers kneeled and bowed before us. I kind of liked being emperor of Rome.

"Pretty cool, huh?" I whispered to Taylor. "Look at me. I'm Caesar, the most powerful man on earth!"

"And I'm Marc Antony, your best friend," Taylor said, smiling.

We both laughed. But we weren't laughing for long.

We soon found that even the most powerful man on earth could run into problems at a place called the Hall of Records.

"I'm sorry, Caesar," a terrified clerk told me, his voice shaking. "But there's no one named Wackerman in the files of Rome. Please, sir! I'm so sorry! Forgive me! But, uh, you see, Wackerman is not a Roman name, my lord! There is no one in all this city who calls himself by such a curious name as Wackerman."

Taylor and I looked at each other, stunned.

This was not good.

Not good at all!

If no Wackermans lived in ancient Rome, then the Confederate spy must have lied about the Wackerman family history.

The original evil Wackerman who owned slaves wasn't even alive in 50 BC — during the time of Julius Caesar.

And we had no idea where, in all of history, to look for the villain we desperately needed to destroy!

Chapter Twenty

I could see that the Roman clerk was afraid I would have him beheaded for defying the orders of his emperor.

I had demanded information from him about a slave owner named Wackerman. But this clerk couldn't help me — *me*, the mighty Julius Caesar.

This was a serious offense in ancient Rome.

But the clerk was lucky, because I wasn't really Caesar, of course. And I knew he wasn't to blame for anything.

He was right, really: Wackerman wasn't a Roman name.

Taylor and I should have realized that earlier.

I tried to use my powers of logic to look for a solution to this new difficulty. After a few moments, something occurred to me.

Sure, it was possible the Confederate spy had

lied about our family's past, but he really had no reason to lie. So it seemed more likely that he had told the truth.

There could be another explanation for all the confusion at the Hall of Records, I decided.

Maybe my family had simply had a different name centuries before arriving in America from Europe — a Roman name. It was worth a try anyway.

"I understand you, clerk," I said. "Do not worry. You are not at fault. Your emperor is not angry. But I wonder if you could help us with another question?"

"Yes, my lord! Anything! Thank you, my lord! You are very kind, great Caesar!"

"Can you think of a slave owner in the city whose name is *similar* to Wackerman?" I asked. "Perhaps a Roman name that sounds something like this strange word?"

"Why, yes, Caesar," the clerk said. "It is a man you know well — a man you have cursed in public for the way he treats his family and his slaves. It is Finius Wacerimus, my lord. He is known as the largest and cruelest slaveholder in your empire, as you perhaps remember."

"Then tell us the fastest way to get to his home, clerk, and Marc Antony and I shall be on our way."

The clerk was more than happy to help Julius Caesar and his most loyal soldier, and he gave us directions to the great marble and granite palace of Finius Wacerimus.

As my guards waited outside for us, I pulled aside Marc Antony — uh, I mean Taylor — to talk things over.

"This Wacerimus guy must be the right one, don't you think?" I asked my friend. "He's got to be the most rotten family member, the guy we're looking for in history."

"I'm pretty sure he must be," Taylor said. "Remember that Confederate spy's name? It was Horace Phinias Wackerman. And that middle name sounds just like this Roman slave owner's first name — Finius. That's way too weird a name for this to be a coincidence!"

"You're probably right," I said. "And Wacerimus sounds kind of like a Roman version of Wackerman, doesn't it? He *must* be the guy!"

"But we've got to make sure before we really destroy this guy, right?" Taylor said. "I mean, we wouldn't want to kill the wrong guy. Maybe if we see him, we'll know by the way he looks or something."

"*Kill* him?" I asked, growing upset. "Are you crazy? The psychic didn't say we had to do that!"

"She said we had to destroy him, remember? You know me, Ben. I don't even like to swat a fly. But we can't let this curse stay on your family forever, can we?"

I didn't know what to say.

And I sure didn't know what to do.

We had overcome so many troubles and traveled through so many centuries of history to get this far.

But now I was frozen with dread and fear.

Kill?

Did we really have to *kill* Finius Wacerimus?

I hadn't given a lot of thought to Marlene's instructions before now. I hadn't had any time to consider what she really meant by her words.

But Taylor was right.

Marlene had told us, "You must destroy the

man who is destroying your family!"

What else could she have meant except that we had to kill him?

I couldn't do it, though — I just couldn't!

I was a budding scientist, not an ax murderer.

I used my *brain* to solve problems, not violence. Now I was faced with a terrible problem.

I could either go against everything I believed, and kill Finius Wacerimus.

Or I could let the vicious slave owner live — and seal the doom of my entire family!

Chapter Twenty-One

What could I possibly do to get out of this mess?

I didn't know.

But I understood that the moment of truth had arrived. I knew my parents must be horribly sick back in the present — if they were still alive at all!

There was no time to lose.

I felt sure Taylor and I finally had found the right man from the Wackerman family's past. This *had* to be the guy who had started so much evil, the guy who had brought the curse upon us Wackermans.

Now, I had to either do it or not do it: destroy Wacerimus or let him live.

But I also felt inside me that neither of those choices was the right one. I couldn't kill him. And I couldn't let him live.

That was when I thought about my friend Taylor, and the awful choice he had faced when I was dying at his house.

Remember that? He'd had to decide whether to mix the time travel antidote while I died before his eyes — or to send me back into history with no way home.

And I recalled that Taylor had found another choice between those two extremes. He had ripped the antidote formula from the book and taken it on our journey into history.

He had saved my life and saved us from wandering around the past forever.

So maybe — just maybe — there was another choice now.

As Taylor stood watching me, I sat down on a marble bench and began to think.

I thought about this problem for minutes and then more minutes and then more minutes still.

I sweated and fretted and stewed over it.

Then, at last, I had an idea!

Marlene the psychic had told us only that we had to "destroy" the evil Wackerman family member. But you don't have to kill a person to destroy him, I reasoned.

Finius Wacerimus was a rich man who depended on slaves to run his business, whatever that business was. If we freed his slaves, we would destroy his business — and allow those innocent people to escape his cruelty.

Surely this would end the evil things Wacerimus was doing. Surely this also would end the curse on the Wackerman family.

"Come on!" I said to Taylor, smacking him on the back. "I know what we can do to destroy Wacerimus and still not harm a hair on his head! I'll explain it on the way!"

With the Roman guards at our side, we hurried back to Caesar's palace in our chariots as dozens of Roman citizens shouted and waved in the streets.

"Hail Caesar! Greetings Antony!" they yelled, bowing and kneeling.

I hardly noticed them because I was busy telling Taylor about my plan.

"Wow, you're a genius, Ben! What a great idea!" he exclaimed after I gave him the details. "I can't wait to see the look on the face of Finius Wacerimus when we show up!"

At the emperor's palace, I assembled three legions of Roman soldiers — each legion being a group of about 3,000 soldiers — all dressed in full battle gear. Helmets, swords, spears, shields.

Then we began to march in grand columns of soldiers towards the palace of the evil Finius Wacerimus.

We looked impressive. Four lines of soldiers stretched out for more than a mile.

No one would dare stand in the way of an army this powerful — the greatest, strongest, toughest army in the world in 50 BC.

When we arrived, I was amazed at the splendor of the Wacerimus palace. It was full of courtyards and gardens and fountains. Every building was made of highly polished marble.

This palace was more beautiful than the home of Caesar himself.

I could also see that Wacerimus was a big-time farmer. His home was surrounded by hundreds of acres of rich, hilly fields, full of olive trees and vineyards.

In these fields, hundreds of slaves toiled and sweated to harvest the crops.

It was a ghastly sight! Human beings were treated like cattle. Men, women and children were whipped and cursed and kicked for no reason.

It was time to cut down this branch of the Wackerman family tree once and for all!

I ordered my soldiers to break the chains that bound the ankles of the slaves.

"Use your strongest swords on those chains!" I commanded. "Tell every slave he or she is free to go! If they choose, they may follow us to the emperor's palace where they will receive food and money from Rome to start new lives!"

The soldiers looked at me strangely.

"Go!" I shouted. "Free every slave owned by Finius Wacerimus! And let no one stand in your way!"

With a flourish of golden trumpets, the troops fanned out among the fields, hacking away the chains. I smiled as I heard wave after wave of wild cheers from the slaves.

"We are free! We are free at last!" they shouted. "Hooray! Hail Caesar!"

I looked at Taylor — you know, the fake Marc Antony — who was watching proudly from the chariot beside me.

"I really want to meet this Wacerimus guy," he said with a laugh. "I've got to see his face. He must be so angry right now!"

That's when I felt it.

The razor-sharp tip of a silver spear was pointed directly at my throat! Someone had crept up behind us as Taylor and I looked across the fields at our troops.

"There is no need to look for Finius Wacerimus," said the man holding the spear. "I am here! Yes, go ahead and laugh at me now, Antony! Hmmmm? Wacerimus will have his revenge for the insult you do me — freeing my slaves! You have destroyed me! Destroyed me totally! But I shall soon destroy something too! In a moment, I will push this spear into the body of great Caesar! He will die in a pool of his own blood — and there is nothing you can do to stop me!"

Chapter Twenty-Two

I turned my head just enough to see Finius Wacerimus out the corner of my eye.

I couldn't believe what I saw.

He looked almost exactly like my teacher, Mr. Wicker — and that Confederate spy, Horace Phinias Wackerman!

Wacerimus was very tall and very skinny. His thin black hair was swept forward around his forehead like a crown, in the Roman style. He had a tiny mustache and a stubby, crooked nose and his black toga was too short.

This was *definitely* the man who had started all the family problems. I felt sure of that.

But who was going to destroy who?

"If I am to die today, so be it!" I said boldly to Wacerimus. "But you should know that my soldiers could have killed you, and did not. I wanted to spare

113

your blood."

"You have spared nothing!" Wacerimus shouted. "I am destroyed! Ruined! You have freed all my slaves! Every one of them is gone!"

"You are an evil man," I said, "And you also fathered an evil family that owned slaves for centuries. But now that will not happen, Wacerimus. Whether you kill me or not, your slave-owning days are over! And your family — *my* family — is free of your curse!"

"Your family?" Wacerimus said, puzzled. "What do you mean your family?"

At that instant, Marc Antony tugged on the reins of his chariot. Of course, it was really my good friend, Taylor, trying to help me.

His horse jerked to the side, slamming into Wacerimus.

The slave owner fell to the ground, dropping his spear. Taylor and I jumped off our chariots and grabbed Wacerimus's arms as soldiers hurried to assist us.

"Take him away and lock him up!" I ordered. "We will not harm this man. But we will teach him to do an honest day's work. He will earn his supper with his own sweat now. No longer will he make poor slaves work so that he may be rich."

The soldiers tied the hands of Finius Wacerimus and led him away in a chariot towards the center of Rome.

"That's it!" Taylor shouted. "We've done it, Ben! We've broken the curse! Thanks to you, we found a way to destroy your evil ancestor without killing him."

"Well, after all, Taylor, this guy was my great-great-great-great-great-great-uncle or something like that," I said. I reached under my belt and pulled out the page with the formula for the antidote on it. "But now we've got to mix up this antidote stuff and get back home. I need to find out how Mom and Dad are doing! I just pray they survived long enough for us to break the family curse!"

"And I hope we can find all the ingredients we need," Taylor said, frowning. "What if the formula needs some medieval stuff like the eyes of newts or something that didn't exist in ancient Rome? I didn't have time to read the formula before I tore the page out."

"Well, if that were true, we could just travel to Medieval times and make the antidote there," I said. "But I've already read the formula and we're in luck. All we need is salt and water. That's it! Any Roman home would have those things. I even remember that the English word *salt* comes from a word used in Roman times."

I don't know how I knew that but I did. Not bad for a guy who doesn't like history, huh?

We hopped on our chariots and shook the reins. Our horses darted off down the road that led to Wacerimus's palace.

We jumped off our chariots the moment we arrived at the door and ran towards the kitchen. On our way, we passed dozens of Roman soldiers who looked confused to see Julius Caesar and Marc Antony racing around like crazy men.

We must have looked pretty silly in our togas, sprinting side by side at a full gallop.

"Remember, Centurion, make sure all the freed slaves get food and money!" I reminded a Roman officer as we passed. "I may have to leave Rome for a while now. You must help carry out my orders!"

"Yes, Caesar!" the officer answered with a Roman salute.

In the kitchen, we found a jar of salt on a marble counter. I grabbed it and a bucket of water. Then I read the antidote formula out loud.

"We'll be home in no time," I said. "It says, 'Take two pinches of salt and add them to one handful of water. Then drink,' Go ahead, Taylor, get some water in your hand. Then I'll drop two pinches of salt in it."

We each scooped up water in the palm of one hand. I reached with my other hand into the salt jar.

"One pinch, two pinches for you," I said. "And one, two for me."

With that, we both drank every drop of the salty water. Then we waited.

And waited.

And waited.

But nothing happened.

"A-are you sure you read the formula right?" Taylor asked with fear in his voice. "You're s-sure that was two pinches of salt?"

"Y-yes," I replied. "I'm s-sure."

We had done everything exactly according to the formula for the antidote listed in the old book.

But it wasn't working!

No spinning. No time travel.

Nothing!

Taylor and I looked at each other. For the first time, we almost started to cry.

There was nothing we could do now if the antidote didn't work.

We were stuck in ancient Rome for the rest of our lives!

Chapter Twenty-Three

Taylor wiped his eyes and put his hand on my shoulder.

"It'll be OK, Ben," he said, though he did not sound as if it would be OK at all. "It's not so bad in Roman times, I guess. Besides, we still have each other. Even if we, uh, never see our parents again."

"Yeah, I guess you're right," I mumbled. "But now I'll never even know if my parents lived through the curse or not. I really want to go home!"

Then without warning, it began.

I felt like I was spinning around in a swivel chair.

Spinning like nutso!

And everything looked blurry.

And, yeah — I still felt like somebody had one finger up my nose. The antidote was working at last, sending us flying back through time!

119

For some reason, the antidote formula was slower to work than the time travel formula.

Now the woman's voice whispered, "Choose."

Only this time I didn't think about Abraham Lincoln or Julius Caesar or anyone else from history books.

I just thought about me — Ben Wackerman.

Suddenly, there I was standing in my living room. Best of all, Mom and Dad were there too!

"Mom! Dad!" I shouted.

"Benny!" they yelled.

They looked and sounded like themselves again!

I was back home with my family, in my own living room. The curse was gone!

We all hugged and cried and kissed and then hugged some more.

What a relief to be back in the present!

But I had a lot to explain to my parents about this strange experience of time travel and morphing.

I had just started to tell them about everything when we heard a knock on the front door.

My buddy, Taylor, was standing there, smiling broadly.

We high-fived and congratulated each other now, whooping and hollering with joy.

Until I noticed someone standing behind him. I guess must have looked really shocked, because Taylor started laughing.

It was Mr. Wicker, our history teacher! He looked just as geeky as ever — except now he seemed kind of shy and embarrassed or something.

"I saw Mr. Wicker walking to your house at the same time as me," Taylor said. "I think he has something to tell you and your family, Ben. It's about this family curse thing."

"Benjamin, I'm so sorry for the way I treated you during history class," Mr. Wicker began. "And I'm simply shocked that I tried to actually harm you! You're my favorite pupil."

"So what happened, Mr. Wicker?" I asked, confused. "Why did you do it?"

"After I tried to strangle you, I felt I needed help from someone, Benjamin. I ended up talking to the same psychic you boys consulted — Marlene," he said. "She told me that I am a distant relative of your family, Benjamin. One part of our family moved from Italy to

America long ago and became the Wackermans. Another part moved here and became the Wickers."

"Oh!" I exclaimed. "I'm starting to get it now!"

"Marlene told me I suffered from the same family curse as you and your parents. In fact, the curse was awakened because I was your teacher," Mr. Wicker continued. "The curse made me hate you every time I talked about history in your presence, Benjamin. I felt I had to stop you from becoming a famous scientist, as I knew you would one day. After all, a scientist with your genius would surely find some formula to break the family curse."

"So you were trying to protect the curse by killing Ben, right?" Taylor said. "You wanted to make sure he didn't grow up into this great scientist."

"Precisely, Taylor," Mr. Wicker said. "As the curse strengthened, my mind became sicker and sicker. Please, forgive me, Benjamin! I feel so very badly about all of this."

"You couldn't help it, Mr. Wicker," I said. "We all were victims of that curse. I'm just glad it's over. And I'm glad Taylor and I are finally home!"

My parents hugged me again and shook Mr.

Wicker's hand.

"There's just one thing, though, Benjamin," Mr. Wicker said, smiling. "I know you haven't enjoyed studying history. I treated you so poorly that I don't blame you. But your time traveling experience has given you a unique point of view on some famous events of the past."

"Wow, that's the truth," Taylor said.

"So I was wondering if you might consider helping me teach history class now," Mr. Wicker said. "Your schoolmates would certainly enjoy it — and I would be very grateful to you."

"Yeah, Ben — how many kids get to have Abe Lincoln and Julius Caesar teach history class!" Taylor laughed.

"OK, sure. I'll do it," I replied. "On one condition, Mr. Wicker."

"Of course, Benjamin," he said. "Anything you like."

"I want Taylor to teach class with us," I said. "He traveled back into history, too — and Taylor's the only reason my family and I are still alive. Besides, he's my best friend."

Taylor and I looked at each other and smiled.

"Hail, Caesar!" he teased, giving me a Roman salute with his fist.

"Greetings, Antony!" I kidded, returning the salute.

We both laughed. And even though they didn't quite understand our joke, my parents and Mr. Wicker laughed right along with us.